I0520904

THE FURRY DISCO

THE FURRY DISCO

Jo Kearley

COYOTE CREEK BOOKS | SAN JOSÉ | CALIFORNIA

Copyright © 2006, 2017 by Jo Kearley

All rights reserved. No part of this book may be used or reproduced by any means, graphic, electronic, or mechanical, including photocopying, recording, taping or by any information storage retrieval system without the written permission of the publisher except in the case of brief quotations embodied in critical articles and reviews.

First edition 2006. Second edition 2017
Printed in the United States of America

The Furry Disco.—2nd ed.

ISBN-13: 978-1-946647-00-9 (pbk)
ISBN-13: 978-1-946647-01-6 (ebk)

25 24 23 22 21 20 19 18 17   2 3 4 5 6 7

Cover painting and illustrations by Russell Powell
Instagram/pangaeanstudios

Published by Coyote Creek Books
www.coyotecreekbooks.com

TABLE OF CONTENTS

THE FURRY DISCO

A modern day parable for young adults which may be shared with parents, pets, professors, and any being who is searching for an insight into reality—consciously or not.

Fur and Feathers Forever!
For All the Animals I Have Loved

Jo Kearley

FOREWORD

Dear Sensei,

Now that you're snacking and behaving angelically, for once, during your monthly fur trim, I think it's an appropriate time to brief you on reading *The Furry Disco*. Puppies less than a year old—like you—will need some pointers on savoring this new type of treat.

The story pre-dates you, the newest member of the Kearley crew, but I'm sure it will start to sound familiar as we begin to read. It's a modern day parable—that's a tale that teaches you about kindness, morals and being a good puppy—and it follows the adventures of several charismatic characters. In fact, you know of many players already. (A hint: they lived with Jo.) Get ready to tag along with them on a thrilling adventure, beyond the backyard or the park! Jo will show you the "true" identities of canines (that's you), felines, birds, rodents and more. They may seem like simple playmates for pups, but they also moon-light—or work other jobs—as crime solvers, rogues, and philosophers.

Now, a word about words, especially the ones you have trouble barking out. You should know that *The Furry Disco* plays cleverly with words. How might a young pup tackle its witticisms? Simple. Frisk with the words as you do with your toys, and chew, chew, chew! Wrestle with them, scoop them in your mouth, and sample the flavors. Grab them from the page the way you steal toys from others. (I promise you won't get in trouble for snatching words!) The bigger the words, the more mouthwatering you'll find them to be. What new spices can you find? What tasty bits will you discover? I guarantee, with some playing of your own, you'll love how delicious they sound sprinkled into the story.

So the next time you roll on your back, in attempt to offset brattiness, ask for some juicy words. I know, you've just mastered *speak* and are hard at work with *off* and *down*. But think of scrumptious words like *scalawag*, much more delectable than plain *mischief-maker*. Instead of *boldness*, how about *chutzpah*? Or, perhaps, *audacity*?

And, when you arrive at the end of *The Furry Disco* and unearth its wisdom, like finding a gem or hidden chew bone, you have my permission to fly over the furniture, straight into Jo's lap. Go ahead, jump from couch to couch; use the coffee table. She'll forgive this tiny burst of naughtiness if you give her dozens of kisses. Roll over, kiss her cheek; blink your twinkling brown eyes. You must let Jo know, for yourself and for all who are smitten with this critter caper—its suspense, its trounce back to the glitz and glamour of the disco era, and its generous dollups of repartée (that means "clever jokes")—that she moves us as a stellar storyteller, a tremendous teacher, and a matchless mama. Never have I known a human more loving of the young, the sophisticated, the winged, and the pawed (yes, including you).

Sweet kisses,

Stephanie

PROLOGUE

2003

Sierra rushed home from her group play date. She was trying to keep it together but just wanted to cover her head with her paws. Sierra was *so* tired of being teased. What had happened to the "Live and Let Live" mentality? It was like P.E. class all over again. And, why? Just because of her pink nose!

The other yellow Labradors were merciless scoffers. So, she looked like a pointer. Big deal. Only the black Labs were half civil.

Once again she had been chosen last for Tennis Ball Scoop. She needed counseling. And quickly. Sierra was seriously considering giving up Outside Society and embracing "house arrest." To be accepted for whom she was seemed a futile exercise. Her nerves were continually frazzled, and, as a result, the work on her novella—*The Joy of Grabbing Erasers (and the like) in Middle School*—was progressing too slowly.

"What a downer! Please let Euphoric be at the house," she whispered to herself. As luck would have it, he was. Euphoric, Euph for short, an elder feline, was known for his optimism and prudence. Sierra and he got along famously. Euph would arch his back, rub against her, and invite a doggie slurp daily. These beige buddies had heart-to-hearts often.

"Hey, Euph, no more play dates for me!" Sierra blurted.

"Calm down, Blondie, what's wrong?"

"Same old! Same old!"

"That pink-nosed slur?"

"Yup," and Sierra's tail drooped between her legs.

Euph walked deliberately into the kitchen, jumped into the sink, and wet his right paw from the ever-accommodating faucet drip. He smoothed his whiskers. Striking a pedantic pose, he cleared his throat.

"Sierra, it's time to acquaint you with *The Furry Disco*. We're going back some forty-odd years."

"Why? What for? I'd rather listen to my music and block out Reality."

Euph persisted. "Sierra, grow up! This tale will make you feel better. Guaranteed. And, I'll throw in some pup biscuits."

At the thought of treats, Sierra acquiesced. Euph understood. Many a principle has been compromised by a cookie. He, himself, was not immune...

CAST OF CHARACTERS

..... Damon

..... Miss Rat

..... Darling

..... Preppy

..... Midnight

..... Bobby

..... Adam

..... Stella

..... Claude

..... Davis

..... Sharon

..... Sleuth

..... Scheherazade

THE LATE '70s

CHAPTER 1

THE PLAYERS

The Dalmatian called the meeting to order. By a show of paws, he discovered that only two of the council members were not present. Snuffing knowingly, he realized that the guilty guinea pigs had, once again, detoured into the garden adjacent to the main gate. Lack of willpower notwithstanding, Damon decided that the tardy girls would receive two demerits each.

Foremost on the agenda, and that which prompted Damon's impatience, was an impending final vote on the group's decision to venture into a corporate business. It had been with an inordinate amount of pride that the animals gathered around the table had received the option of purchasing "The Furry Disco," centrally located in the downtown mall. The former owners, three Siberian Huskies, had lost their franchise when they had restricted admission to the club to canines only. A class action suit had been brought against them by felines, rodents, and feathered fellows.

Damon felt that after years of tasting discrimination—"spots" have never been considered fashionable—he, although canine, had enough savvy to agree with his other-species friends. Damon's daddy, Champion Hamburger III, had been decidedly disappointed in his offspring, when at the end of his son's official puppyhood, it was discovered that Damon's spots ran into one another. Blotchy spots are a Dalmatian's curse! And, to add insult to injury, these same spots were completely absent on his ears. Sadly, Damon had become the black sheep of the family—if it's proper to refer to a dog as a sheep.

One could easily understand why the animals had chosen him as their CEO. Damon's hyperactive antics were just a façade*—a smoke screen if you will—to cover his inner philosophical yearnings. If one is searching for a "raison d'être*," it's better to pretend to be happy-go-lucky and carefree. It catches others off guard. He had found out long ago that serious thoughts make others uncomfortable.

After a while, Damon had begun to enjoy his antics. He particularly relished, all ninety pounds of him, standing on top of the patio picnic table and cavorting thereupon. "A right paw in, a right paw out…shake it all about." He wasn't exactly the dainty type. Maybe it was the purity of the air—it was worth the risk of a slight nosebleed—or the shocked expressions of his audience that caused his exhilaration. Whatever, the animals adored him.

Damon had appointed Darling his right-hand cat. Rhetoric* was her strong point. A tabby of dubious origins, she exhibited behavior the very opposite of darlingness. Her extreme fury at limitations had caused her to fine tune the art of spitting. She was the liberated female before "The Women's Movement" had taken hold. Darling was proud of her reputation. Indeed, she would not hesitate to bite the hand that fed her.

Her antisocial behavior had developed—and most Freudians* would agree—because of a ghastly kittenhood incident. She had been relaxing on a grey shag-carpeted staircase, blending sublimely into the color scheme, when it had happened. Darling had been stepped on, crushed if you please, by a six foot, two hundred pound human guest who was on his way to the lower level.

There are no words to describe being "totaled"—comic strips like Garfield to this day strain her patience. Darling had crept under a dresser and hovered between life and death for three days and nights. It must have been the tough alley-cat genes that turned the tide. She survived, but her feminine temperament did not!

Her personal credo could best be described as "laissez-faire*." Occasionally she would pretend to tolerate a localized stroking under the chin. Involuntary purring would ensue only to cease abruptly for no apparent cause. Her purrogative. Moreover, Darling was quite proud of the fact that of all those assembled here today, she alone was never bothered by the obnoxious flea. Countless hypotheses had been brought forth to explain this phenomenon. The consensus of opinion was that she was just so mean, her blood so sour, that even this pest was thwarted. It gave her an elevated status in the community.

To her right sat Midnight. No one could figure him out—totally inscrutable cat that he was. If forced to describe him, words such as "exotic" or "mysterious" came to mind. In truth, "creepy" and "shadowy" were the more appropriate adjectives. He had perfected a human-baby cry that would tug at your heartstrings or your tolerance depending on the lateness of the hour. His request to gain entry into the bird room for academic observation was never granted due to his questionable motives. He just wasn't the clean-cut, intellectual type.

One has difficulty describing the oozing, gliding movement Midnight used to traverse a room. To say "stalking" would be most inept. One young koala bear had experienced recurring nightmares for a month, and had fallen off his eucalyptus branch four times, whenever thoughts of his fifth grade field trip to a former council meeting surfaced. The class was studying Introductory Civics, a.k.a. "The Rights and Duties of Citizens." Midnight had delivered a keynote address on elementary or basic cunning. He had scared the youngsters half to death. Consequently, the distraught teacher had sworn off outings for the duration of the semester.

It was rumored that Midnight had a heart of gold under his sinister exterior. History is filled with accounts of outcasts who, because of their looks, had been maligned unjustly. All of Midnight's actions were interpreted negatively. However, his services on the council reflected a certain stoicism*. He, for one, had never flinched when receiving a shot from the veterinarian. His presence balanced the more flighty constituency.

Slouched nearby, hoping to attract minimal attention, was Adam—the most timorous of the felines. He could usually be seen with his right front paw raised off the ground. It was his automatic response to any unusual sound. The trauma of his life had been the California Malathion* Spraying Campaign. The first time he heard the helicopters, certain that his worst fears were being realized, he dive-bombed into the nearest closet and remained hidden for several hours. In other words, courage was not his leading attribute. Adam had heard that the "Meek Shall Inherit the Earth" and was waiting. His facial markings added to his discomfort. Whiskers and coloring blended into one fierce-looking mustache. His countenance at times was quite stern. Appearances can be deceiving. Adam was, at this very minute, being hassled by the last of the feline quartet, Claudius.

Claudius was alternately swiping at Adam's tail and nipping him under the table. Claude, a forever kitten, exhibited all the traits of one who knows that he is adorable and therefore gets away with murder. An overabundance of vanity or conceit was his prime characteristic. He'd plunk down with an angelic "who-me?" pose, fluff out his abnormally bushy tail, and ingratiate his way into your heart. He felt that he was loved by all. His self-assurance led to a secure sense of superiority. Claude even used his name as one example. Follow this: he would never find himself in the dreaded, barbaric predicament of being declawed. For if you were to declaw a Claude, you would be left with a declawed Claude or ultimately just a "de." The "de" couldn't be "he." Such ramblings enabled him to enter the business world as a board member with a voting capacity, for circular reasoning is a prerequisite for such a position.

There was a skirmish at the door. Sharon and Scheherazade, the absentee guinea pigs, came rushing (or rather scooting) across the floor. Sharon, a black satin piggie resembling an eggplant, had greenery dripping from the corners of her mouth. Scheherazade, the more glamorous of the two, long-haired and streaked blonde, might have escaped detection of guilt except for her overwhelming chlorophyll breath when she mumbled, "Hi." Damon glared at them as they seated themselves next to Miss Rat who, with her methodical mind, could never comprehend tardiness.

Miss Rat's beady, pink eyes marked serious disapproval, and her whiskers quivered in disappointment. She felt that her own rodent status was being blemished by these two clumsy girls. Her theory was that by eating their cardboard box shelter once a month, they had somehow affected their brain cells. Miss Rat had never once toyed with the idea of eating her way through a maze, even though that would have enabled her to reach her favorite munchie—an unblanched peanut—much faster. She spent many an hour hanging upside down from her ladder contemplating how she could reroute these two frivolous creatures onto a civilized gnawing course. Miss Rat felt that she had a calling in this direction, visualizing herself as a Florence Nightingale* of Social Work. Her albinism* would even make it unnecessary to buy a nurse's outfit.

Suddenly, an ear-shattering screech assaulted the room. The feather set—three canaries, four parakeets, and six finches chirped in unison at the raucous arrival of their leader. Preppy, the young Lilac Crown Amazon parrot, had been given an equally weighted vote as the felines. This was not surprising in light of the fact that most of his life had been spent on a queen-sized bed with his buddy, Adam. This friendship had been cemented when Preppy realized that he could actually walk over this particular cat, slide down his back, or play "attack-the-tail" with no harmful results to his bird-being. Imagine Preppy's delight when he discovered that at times he could even bully this kitty. However, Prep adopted a protective attitude, and it became quite common to see Adam asleep with a green tuft of feathers napping nearby, one-footed, puffied, one eye slightly opened in order to guard his shy friend.

They were a motley group—those who were present at this meeting.

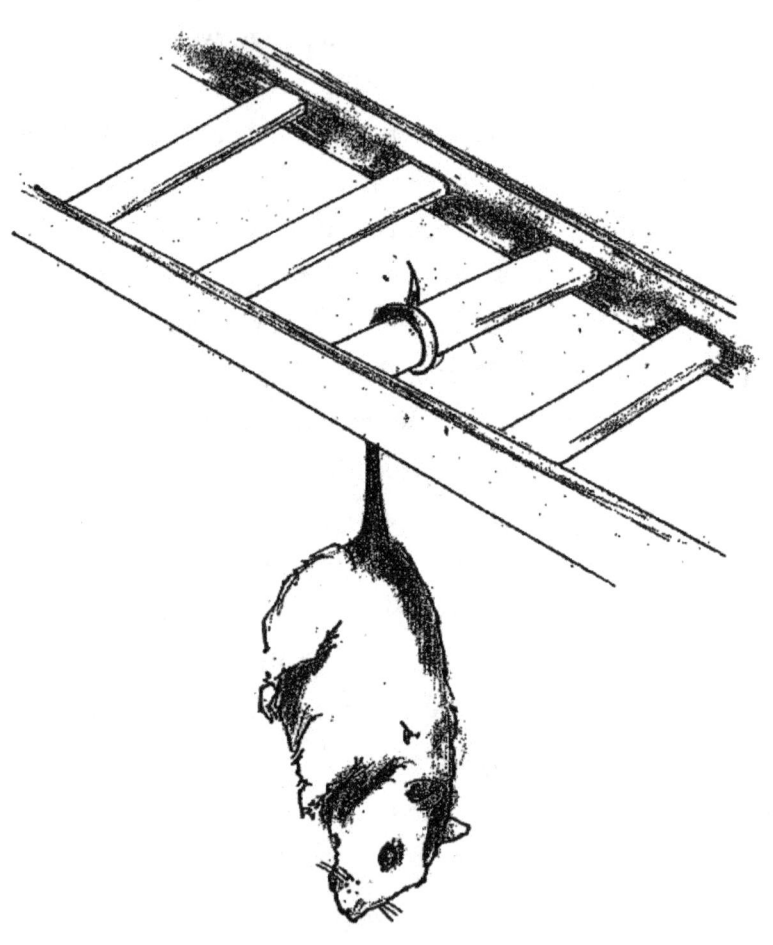

CHAPTER 2

THE BALLOT

Finally the voting was about to commence. Should they, or should they not, purchase "The Furry Disco"? Was it worth the risk? Was this well-thought out or a whim? Damon had to be certain about the degree of sincerity, so he would ask for collateral* if the vote were in the affirmative. He had decided that there were two issues involved here: financial (dollars) and, even more important, personal commitment. Furthermore, instead of an open show of paws, a secret polling had been decided upon. This would help avoid any embarrassment or undue peer pressure. The collateral offerings were to be scanned only by Damon and Preppy. Then they were to be sealed and appropriately buried.

This precautionary hush-hush was essential in order to avoid any inter-species spats. An inadvertent, sarcastic meow at the offer of four unsalted pumpkin seeds as supreme "sealed-in-blood" pledge might cause some discord among the would-be entrepreneurs*. Damon was able to remain stone-faced throughout the ceremonial pledges except for one precarious moment—namely that of Sharon's offering. But now I'm getting ahead of myself. Please note, however, that his amusement was cleverly masked by pretending to have an itch and thumping his tail loudly as an outlet for his mirth.

You, the reader, may look over Preppy's shoulder as he looks over Damon's. Remember, please be open-minded. "Beauty is in the eye of the beholder," and so forth. The tally was as follows:

Darling voted yea. Her collateral was one bronzed slice of kosher salami, commemorative of the day her favors were sought by means of a bribe. The grey-haired lady had wanted to pet her. After all, she had mothered two pampered kitties of her own. So she held out the deli morsel and started the "Here kitty, kitty" routine. Darling did accept the tidbit and then bit the shameless, offending hand. Unfortunately, in the aftermath, her guilty conscience prevented her from actually taking a taste. Darling knew that the elderly woman had meant no harm. Therefore she had had the meat bronzed as a dramatic symbol of her martyrdom*. Darling was fiercely independent but visited occasionally by a scruple or two.

Midnight voted yea. His collateral was one dog-...er...cat-eared Ace of Spades playing card that he had stealthily lifted at Wicked Willie's Magic Show. Said performances were later banned in five major counties. This particular card supposedly enabled the bearer to frighten would-be fortune seekers. It automatically predicted a bleak future, with varying proofs of its authenticity. For instance, so-and-so had lost a valuable diamond-studded collar; so-and-so's entire family had reported electric can opener failure…Midnight had kept it hidden next to his favorite voodoo doll.

Adam voted a tentative yea. He shakingly offered his precious high-frequency dog whistle which he had bought after saving his pennies for three months and giving up tuna treats. He had consistently worn it around his neck, just in case. What if there were an earthquake? What if a kitten were lost? His qualms were overcome when Adam realized that if their business venture were successful, he could afford a head-to-tail security system on a twenty-four hour basis. His heart rate accelerated at the very thought.

Claudius voted yea. Dubbed "Mr. Arrogant" by his peers, he nevertheless conceded his cherished whisker comb as collateral. His were the pawprints on all the mirrors in the house. Claude just couldn't resist those self-admiring glances. He figured that he would give up his macho image and favor the rough, outdoor look for the time being. Anyways, he was breaking in another brush surreptitiously.

Scheherazade voted yea. She donated a four-inch square of pressed cardboard. Said collateral was a cherished chunk of the very first box she had ever eaten. It seemed like only yesterday that she had taken a tiny nibble on a dare and had found the texture irresistible. The piece symbolized her "coming-out," if you will. She heard strains of "Let's Get Physical" each time she looked at it. A tear ran down her cheek as she handed it over.

Sharon voted yea. Her controversial collateral were two wilted parsley sprigs—former residents in a veggie patch— entwined with a red band. The sprigs were reminders of that memorable day when Sharon had lost all self-control, cast temperance to the wind, and had wallowed in a vegetarian frenzy. Scheherazade had had to forcibly remove her from this grassy spree. For a full year afterwards, Sharon was required to wear a matching scarlet ribbon as penance for her actions. Damon's tail was metronoming at this moment. Ah-hem.

Miss Rat voted a reluctant yea and offered her very own Ultimate Maze Solution encased in a Master Peanut Shell. She was proud of her research. In fact, she had delivered many a guest lecture at various university gatherings on how to deal with daily, diverse, dutiful drudgery as defined within the larger, more complex, dilemma of domesticity. Quite a mouthful that.

Preppy voted a collective yea for the bird lobby. That day in San Francisco had been wonderful. His collateral was a seed-coated earring, removed post and all, from under the girl's ringlets. The teen, while touring San Francisco, had arrived at Pier 39 and wanted an authentic parrot-on-shoulder, pirate-fashion photo. Prep had been more than happy to oblige. And, he had felt justified in taking this tiny doodad. Thereafter Prep enjoyed the process of dipping the earring in honey and rolling it in sundry varieties of seed. Encasing memorabilia was his favorite hobby.

Damon made it unanimous. His own personal pledge was backed by his treasured baby blankee. His image would be ruined if the others knew that his old puppy-ties still existed. Lipstick stains adorned one end of the blanket—still visible after countless washings—an indelible reminder of the day he was kissed by "The Woman." Suffering the humiliation of being black, white, and red all over! Trying to wash his blankee and succeeding only in smearing every stain! Now, whenever he noticed a certain wistful look in a woman's eye, he ran for cover.

Damon dug a large hole under a weeping willow outside the council room. Preppy methodically dropped the valued items in, waiting a respectful interval between each one. In order to fill in the opening, Damon used his famous double-back kick. He didn't want to be embarrassed again. Preppy had teased him at the onset of the burial when, momentarily forgetting that he was not alone, Damon had used his nose to engineer the hole as expeditiously as possible. No self-respecting Dalmatian can stand being compared to a well-known snouted barnyard animal.

"The Furry Disco" now belonged to them.

CHAPTER 3

THE STAFF

There were so many nitty-gritty decisions to make that Damon found out if he thought about it too long, it became mind-boggling. Therefore he decided to be super-organized and write a list of priorities. The immediate council group would fulfill all the major posts. Damon was going by the rule of paw that the best policy was one of keeping "outsiders" to a minimum. The one exception was going to be Bobby the kangaroo—hereafter referred to as Bobby the Bouncer. Since the disco was to be a profit-making undertaking, inasmuch as money was to pass paws so to speak, Bobby's worth as a guard was all too apparent.

Bobby had been in the U. S. of A. for several months now,

after having served a stint as a Qantas steward. He had been seeking other employment since that fateful, stormy flight when he had clumsily—and quite without design—trip-hopped onto an elderly matron's lap while serving her a Seven-Up. A fizzing disaster ensued! Seven-Up down and Bob up—on passenger! He had, needless to say, never fully regained his composure. As a consequence of this incident, he had been officially relegated to the microwave/heating detail. Sometimes he had been allowed to demonstrate the safety equipment—but only stationed up front away from the travelers.

Actually, Damon had first met Bobby while browsing at "The International Supermarket." Bobby was demonstrating "speed-cooking" between flights. He was working for extra credits to be applied towards his culinary degree. Terra firma* was his goal. His exhibition was Australian stew à la bone, prepared and heated in two minutes flat. Damon had not invested in a microwave but had embraced a friendship with Bobby. They were often to be seen together on pleasant afternoons playing soccer. Not surprisingly, Bobby's picnic spreads were magnificent. Bobby was delighted when Damon telephoned and offered him the disco job at ten dollars an hour. Visions of aprons and chef's hats overwhelmed him. He jounced for joy!

Damon and Preppy, when finished with the delicate task of delegating duties, called upon Darling to post the list. She was to hang around, eavesdrop, and report any undue negativity. However, the strategic placements were so well-planned that all personnel were pleased with their assignments. The "insiders" would be kept quite busy, if even a fraction of their expectations were met.

Damon, as host or maître-d', had chosen Preppy as his liaison parrot, a.k.a. communication guide. Darling and Midnight would be stationed at the front door. Midnight was the cashier and would collect the five dollar cover charge. In the mood-darkened environment, his blackness blending into the aura, his green phosphorescent eyes would surely intimidate any would-be gate-crashers. It was hoped that the cover charge would discourage any undesirable element.

Darling, on the chair by his side, would supervise I.D. control. She would stamp paws or tail feathers. Hers would be the final word—if the dress code had been adequately met. This meant evening collars for the critters and formal leg bracelets for the feathered crowd. Whether or not Midnight and Darling would be able to work harmoniously together was an unknown. They had managed to co-exist in one household for nine years— although not necessarily side by side.

Adam, in a state of mini-shock, had just learned that he would be the bartender. Preppy was reassuring him that all would go well. "B...but why m...me? I will have to constantly be meeting strangers, Prep."

"Listen, Adam, you are without a doubt, the most reliable when it comes to lacing drinks with just the right amount of catnip. Yours is the most honorable paw-measure."

"Still Prep, I...d...don't..."

Preppy's eyes suddenly brightened, and he fluffed out his tail feathers.

"Adam, I've got a great idea. Bobby will be stationed right next to you at the bar—only a hop away. He will be right there if you need him!"

Adam reluctantly agreed. Nevertheless, he was not convinced that he could endure the entire nerve-racking scene.

On the other hand, Claudius was effervescent. He could barely contain his joy when he saw himself listed as the country-western D.J.

Darling, being facetious, asked him, "Would you prefer to be called Dick Claude?"

"Right on, Darling! D.C. as D.J.! Moi—a cool cat!"

Darling walked away with a condescending spit. These males were a bit too hard to take. She watched Claude exit and strut towards the boutique down the street. She pitied the poor salesperson who would try to accommodate his demands. Mr. Smooth would never be able to choose the ultimate cowboy outfit. Darling would send Midnight to collect him, if he hadn't returned in five hours.

Of the three rodents, guess which two were dancing in circles! Absolutely correct! The wistful waitresses! Sharon and Scheherazade were oh-so-anxious to don their Parisian mini-aprons. And, the thought of those leafy tips!

"Aren't you excited, Miss Rat?" queried Scheherazade.

Miss Rat, in a rather severe tone, reminded her that manners forbade any teenage-show of emotion. Yes, she was pleased, albeit calm, to be designated "Miss Hidden Camera." Those years of hanging upside-down had finally paid off. She couldn't believe that now she would actually be paid for her observations.

"What about all the birdies, girls?" Miss Rat inquired. "What kind of stints were they assigned?"

Sharon retorted in a high-pitched tone. "Ah, Miss Rat, Damon is sooo clever! The feather crew is to take charge of the interludes between records. Preppy has nicknamed them 'Intermittent Intermissionites'—quite a whistleful!"

All in all, appointments were rated an unqualified success.

CHAPTER 4

THE AMBIANCE

The next day Damon gathered the group together and expounded on the projected physical layout of the disco. It was with a great deal of pride that he announced several innovations.

"Okay, guys and gals, here goes! Listen sharply! I'll start from the middle and work outwards. In the center, there will be a circular dance floor shaped like a huge, white…uh…spot." He ignored a few titters from the audience. "Strobe lighting, will produce, I hope, a giddying effect. The dizzy, dancing customers will become happy hoofers, although in the profound sense 'dizzy' is not necessarily synonymous with 'happy.' Although…"

Preppy flew quickly to Damon's shoulder and hurriedly

reminded him that he must not sidetrack into ideology at this point. So he continued.

"Small tables, seating three to four, will be placed in semicircle fashion around the sp…uh…the dance floor. There will, however, be a few recessed booths for privacy. To be sure, there will be a 'squeaking' and a 'non-squeaking' section to separate the vociferous* from the melancholic. Although sometimes the meaning of…" A glare from Prep kept him from continuing. But oh—it was a temptation almost beyond his doggie-control.

After a few deep snuffs, Damon resumed. "I will hang over the counter-bar, on the wall opposite the D.J.'s platfor—" whereupon Claude couldn't resist taking a bow, "in the place of honor, my priceless original recording of the Beagles singing their splendid solid gold hit 'Puppy Love.'" Sharon and Scheherazade almost swooned at this point, much to Miss Rat's disgust.

"Remember friends, this song was number one on the charts for a startling nine months in the early sixties. My uncle, Chief Spot, received it, along with an engraved trophy, for his heroism while serving in Firehouse 409. He had single-pawedly rescued two elderly Siamese. The damsels, seemingly trapped under a velvet sofa due to a neglected candle tipping over and igniting the drapes, awaited succor. The ladies, who were quite tired of the youth-oriented society, were having an old-fashioned tea party, doilies and all, that memorable evening." Damon had a faraway-look in his eye as he continued.

"There was that moment of truth, when Uncle smashed

through the apartment door. At that very instant, he cough-ingly—smoke was everywhere—uttered those famous words which were to become every rookie Dalmatian's credo."

At this point, Damon asked them all to rise while, with his paw over his heart, he quoted solemnly, "Singed spots are a small price to pay for the saving of a life."

The audience was visibly moved. Even Claude took out his newly purchased silk hanky and blew his nose twice, once out of necessity and once for dramatic effect. Preppy had to remind Damon to reseat his public.

Damon began to elucidate on the décor. However, he asks you, the reader, to be patient and not listen in. He believes in building up momentum towards opening night. Use your imagination. Damon feels that "Anticipation is sometimes greater than the event, although…"

The excitement was palpable.

CHAPTER 5

Pre-Opening

A month of determined preparation had passed. There had been the usual minicatastrophes: a broken glass, a delayed carpenter, a sulky black cat. Midnight's blues were prompted by Damon's "Honesty is the best policy" constant refrain. As Midnight had told Claude, "A little purr-loining on the side wouldn't really hurt anyone."

Claude had had to remind him that Damon was not the type one disobeyed. "Besides, Midnight, didn't your mama warn you as a kitten about cat burglars?"

Adam, overhearing the last word only, sprinted under the nearest table. Preppy, shaking his feathers, advised the crew that there should be less chitchat and more work. Only Miss Rat seconded his motion. She definitely found most conversations to be expendable. Soon they were all caught up in the magnitude of the happening. Tiresome chores and emotional worry.

Before long it was the morning of opening night. For "Time and Tide wait for no animal," as Damon put it.

Preppy and his group of attendants (a royal retinue) had devised, after weeks of deliberation, a publicity gimmick which was about to be launched. They were going to release one hundred balloons, white with black lettering. "Popping"? "Popping Open"? "Opening Pops"? "Pop Open"? "Opening Pop"? The message, they had bickeringly decided upon, was "The Furry Disco Pops!" Preppy had felt that adding "open" to "pops" would have been redundant. In fact, the finches and parakeets had had a "seedy" fight over the matter. Never again would they be allowed in the public relations department!

Anyway, one, and only one, balloon would sport a huge purple spot under the writing. The finder of this particular balloon was to receive complimentary admission to the gala festivities, as well as personalized photo with Damon to highlight the evening and serve as a cherished keepsake of the star-studded night.

It was a rather pedestrian* promotional stunt to be sure but none-the-less effective with the animal populace. Preppy had advised the newspapers of the event. Joseph, the panda, the cub reporter assigned to cover this entertainment milestone, promised the lucky "purple-spot" winner a three-line quote of his or her choice. There is not a critter alive who could be indifferent when it came to seeing his, or her, words in print.

It was nearing high noon. The birds were in formation. They hovered above like a wayward cloud. Clean-up crews had been hired to remove any deflated balloons immediately. Environmental safety regulations required it. The flock cast loose the spheres. A few minutes later, Preppy himself let go of the purple-spotted prize. He dropped it, by design, over the bustling thoroughfare on Main Street. Animals from all walks of life were pursuing their Friday routines, running errands, and meeting lunch dates. In his heart, Preppy wanted a blue-collar worker to be the winner. He felt that the experience would be a bit more meaningful if it were unprecedented and interrupted a daily grind.

The special balloon drifted drowsily downwards. The birds tittered with elation. Slowly, slowly—and the lucky recipient was Stella, the aardvark!

She was "daylighting" that fateful morning as a vacuum cleaner in order to augment her dwindling savings. She had squandered too many a dollar on mail-order ant farms. Stella, a single mom with two hungry pre-teens to feed, had decided that cleaning duties were just up her snout. She had been on her way to her first assignment, a coffee shop with dense foliage, when she had been tapped on the head by The Balloon.

She couldn't believe it. Lady Luck had never visited her before. Bowing to Fate, Stella made an instantaneous decision. She stopped short, turned around, and retraced (with a skip) her steps home, all the while clasping the balloon snugly. She needed an afternoon of rest and beautifying. After all, how many ladies wouldn't give their right paw to have a picture taken with Damon? Or even just to be in the same room? He was so intellectual and so handsome! A sweet combination! Joy gave way to quandary when she realized the implications of her actions. She had never, in her entire life, missed a day of work before. Well, she…she would call in sick, which wasn't really a lie since she really was! Sick with anticipation that is!

We shall give Stella her privacy. Not we, who would intrude upon the delicate activities adopted by female aardvarks as an assurance of appearing at their very best. Vague notions of mud packs, armor-perms, and mascara can float through our minds. Suffice it to say, Stella spared no expense for this once-in-a-lifetime opportunity.

The moment was approaching.

CHAPTER 6

ALMOST THERE

It was one exquisite aardvark who approached "The Furry Disco" that evening. Intoxication was rampant. A line, a full block and a half long, had already queued* up. Ebullience was contagious; spirits were high. It was nearly 8:00 p.m., yet the atmosphere reeked of high noon.

Two patrol officers had been assigned to the immediate area, just in case the crowd became unruly. The cops were Saint Bernards, and their individual tails kept the collective one in place. After all, the tale of being whiplashed by a tail is too titillating for any self-respecting animal to tolerate, even if it is tailored in the telling.

Stella's heart began to pound with excitement. She stepped to the front of the line, oblivious to the cries of "No cuts!" and showed her pass—a.k.a. "The Balloon." Preppy was summoned.

As his first official liaison duty, Prep flew off to inform Damon that the "P.R." guest of honor had arrived.

"P.R.! P.R.!" he screeched. "Proud Recipient! Proud Recipient!"

A quintet of macaws in line happily joined the chant.

Prep alerted Midnight to the fact that the "VIP freebie" had just appeared and to usher her in when the doors opened.

Midnight "humphed" only once. He remembered the "humphing" camel's punishment from Rudyard Kipling's Just So Stories. He, the most superstitious of them all, didn't quite believe the consequence, and yet, on the other paw, didn't want to test the theory out. He could wind up a stock boy just chewing his cud. He made no further comment.

All in all, Midnight was already taking his financial duties a mite too seriously. Therefore, even one complimentary cover fee was nigh impossible for him to visualize, let alone handle. Where-oh-where had his stoical attitude gone? The fact that he had been dreaming about frozen assets alongside of frozen flounder for the past fortnight seemed some sort of sign.

Darling, having overheard the unintentional "humph," remarked demurely, "Be careful, Midnight. Your slyness is starting to resemble Midasness*."

"Listen, Darling, back off! I know why you're so smug. Our winner is a pink-collared she. You consider that quite a masterstroke, don't you?"

Darling nodded her assent. She was absolutely delighted that a female, albeit an aardvark (the latter species not particularly credited with media appeal), had become the disco's first celebrity guest.

Feminists needed all the help they could get these days.

CHAPTER 7

THE OPENING

The disco's doors were officially unlocked. The customers entered. Damon awaited Stella at the end of the hall. Having been prepped by Prep, he had accordingly assumed an avuncular* posture. It was a stance that Damon had used before. In his younger days, he had indeed searched for romance. Unfortunately, the outcome of that particular quest had been a disaster. He had sworn off "l'amour" accordingly. Damon reminisced.

The young lady who had once captured his heart, Fifi, a flirtatious French poodle, had sworn her eternal love. She had willingly accepted his favors and gifts over a period of several months. Damon had looked forward to a Hallmark happily-ever-after future. However, since she was secretly social climbing, Fifi (at her first opportunity) ran off with an auburn Afghan hound who proclaimed links to nobility (of dubious origins at that).

Damon had been left a *Dear Damon...er...John** letter. Thank you for everything, but good luck and good bye! No hard feelings. Nothing personal. The usual text. Damon had subsequently renounced all Europeans (dogs do adhere to vast generalizations). Ergo, he quite welcomed the chance to escort an African lady through the revelry of opening night. He sighed heavily and stepped forward.

Stella saw Damon wave his paw and barely kept from fainting. He was even more handsome in person. She took a deep breath and allowed herself to be ushered into "The Furry Disco" itself.

It took a moment or two for her eyes to adjust to the darkness. But then, it was Serendipity* and Shangri-La* rolled into one! The well-kept secret concerning the décor was startlingly revealed. It was authentic Wild West. Urbanity thrown to the wind!

The bar was horse-shoe shaped; the bar stools were saddled. Two giant cacti bordered each end, upon which several of the feather contingent had positioned themselves. Finches one side! Keets the other! The canaries, the most sensitive of the group, rocked placidly on a golden swing suspended overhead. The fluorescent bulb had lulled them into thinking they were in Mexican moonlight. Their mild chirpings and warbles were quite muffled in the increasing din of partying animalkind. A flashing neon light, in rhythm with sporadic gunshot effects, illuminated the symbol of their dream—Damon's prized Beagles' record.

Accompanied by Damon, Stella felt like Annie Oakley* herself.

CHAPTER 8

"And So It Begins..."

Damon and Stella seated themselves at a booth adjacent to the mini-stage. Nearby, Joseph, overwrought by the occasion, discovered much to his chagrin that he had forgotten his pen. He blanched furiously when he was forced to borrow a writing utensil from a black Labrador retriever, Junior Jowls. Damon was visibly amused by this particular exchange. Junior, anxious to help, checked his bag of sticks. An honorable Lab is never without his personal stick-supply. After all, if one is so attached to wooden objects of a certain shape, it is best not to be left at the mercy of destiny. Ditto for tennis balls.

In this particular instance, Junior came up empty-pawed. However, he felt so much compassion for the distraught cub that he, in turn, managed to succeed in borrowing a pen from Midnight.

As Midnight himself declared, "I have a weakness for large dogs who fearlessly defy Nature in order to retrieve, ignominiously or not, sodden or not, that which is thrown into water!"

"Why is that?" asked Junior.

"Well, I will never forget the day that I slipped into the tub while I was swiping at errant bubbles floating from the bubbly bath. There I was, sitting on the rim, more precariously balanced than I thought, when *splash!* May I be frank, Junior?"

An emphatic "Of course!"

"The unpleasant sensation of wet fur, the mildewed dry-ing-out process, the entire nerve-racking experience left me forever in awe of any working water dog. I even purchased a framed portrait of a golden retriever…er…no offense, Junior. My color scheme at that time reflected a pawcity of pallid pastels. I hung it on my bedroom wall."

Junior nodded his head. Although to be quite honest, the entire perception of Water as anything but wonderful was beyond his understanding. In fact, he shook his ears several times, on the way back to Joseph, in an attempt to comprehend this unfamiliar viewpoint. As for taking offense at the "golden" remark, it was the furthest thing from his mind. Junior had been brought up to believe that "Black is Beautiful!" And, that was that.

Joseph thanked him for the pen and kept Stella and Damon

in view. He had decided to record all his impressions and worry about editing later. Joe jotted down that Stella seemed "psyched-out," most likely due to her state of bliss. To quote, "Her snout, at this moment, is totally incapable of sucking-in even the plumpest ant—had the Olympic contender presented himself." Joseph was quite proud of his prose.

Damon, with a slightly bemused facial expression, decided to order Stella a Shirley Temple. He excused himself and walked towards the bar. He gestured to Adam.

The night was moving in the right direction.

CHAPTER 9

REFRESHMENTS AND A NEW EMPLOYEE

Adam was already experiencing difficulty in keeping up with the voracious collective thirst that had developed due to his generous paw's measure of catnip and his sympathetic ear. Adam, good-natured feline that he was, listened attentively to his customers' life stories and soon gained the nickname of "Benevolent One." He was beginning to feel that he had a Ph.D. in Psychology, so coveted was his advice. His former tottering ego began to swell with each blessing, thanks, or forever-grateful-for-your-opinion remark. He expected the orders to slow down a bit after the dancing started.

One of these kind listening sessions resulted in an unexpected friendship. It happened like this. After a few tears shed into his mango juice, Davis, a blue-front Amazon, stopped his incoherent sobbing between beakfuls to tell Adam his tale of woe.

"I was...*sniff*...transported from Mexico and quarantined with twenty others. It was beyond boring and not the most pleasant situation to be in." Davis paused to snuff twice. "So, in order to amuse myself, I learned how to wolf-whistle. I had been naively unaware that no self-respecting, capable-of-talking parrot, should ever toy with this inferior form of communication."

Adam refilled his glass, no charge of course, and urged him to continue. He motioned Bobby over to hear the rest of this narrative.

Davis resumed, "I enjoyed the coos murmured by all females within earshot of my whistles. The coy bobbing of flattered heads. And, everything was fine 'til one day—what was I thinking?—I forgot myself and wolf-whistled while two crows were perched nearby. They immediately took it upon themselves to broadcast my compromising faux pas* via their caustic, cantankerous calling. And I, Davis, was thereby excommunicated from the flock."

Adam hesitated, "You mean you're...?"

"Yes, at this time, I'm totally without perch and board."

And Davis started to hiccup in an attempt to swallow his sobs.

After punctuating his condolences with understanding purrs, Adam came up with a short term solution to Davis's dilemma.

"Listen, Davis. Would you like to be Preppy's assistant? I'm sure you'd qualify."

"Are you positive?" asked Davis, his tail feathers starting to spread.

"Absolutely! We have lots of dispatches to deliver. And, best of all, in case of a dire emergency, you can give a superduper shriek as an alarm.

"One can never be too safe," Adam murmured under his whiskers.

Davis became so excited at this point that he whistled on the spot, much to the nearby customer's annoyance. Then, suddenly inspired, he demonstrated his raucous jungle cry. The screech was so unexpected that two chinchillas fell off their barstools in sheer panic, thereby dislodging their cache* of raisins stuffed under the pommel. This so amused three observant lop-eared bunnies, tickled their fancy so to speak, that it was not long before they, too, were lop-sided as well as lop-eared—from laughing, of course. Snicker to guffaw. Shamefacedly on the floor next to the chinchillas, no longer lapped on stool, but lopped under!

Davis, having inadvertently created his own mini-crisis, sounded his alarm. Preppy, security officer extraordinaire, came flying to assess the damage. He decided that it was a case of bruised egos rather than battered bodies. The bunnies and chinchillas avoided each other's eyes for the rest of the evening.

After Adam had explained, in almost apologetic tones, his idea about Davis, Preppy agreed to try it out for a probationary period of two to three weeks. Perch and board would take the place of an hourly wage. Davis almost wolf-whistled in delight but caught himself just in time.

CHAPTER 10

Cool D.J. and Scheherazade's Woe

Abruptly, the room darkened, and the spotlight shone. Claude was making his grand entrance. He was magnificently accoutered in knee-high cowboy boots, Cat City jeans, and long-sleeved silk shirt. Around his neck, he wore a red bandanna; on his head sat a splendid western hat. As the final touch, a gold-plated cufflink adorned the base of his tail. Claude was one smooth dude!

Unfortunately, in his zeal, he had over-doused himself with cologne ("Brute") for that ultra-masculine allure. The result of this misplaced action was that several moments of "angry-skunk" panic had ensued. Customers were holding their noses and trying to breathe through their mouths. Two out-of-town visiting Petit Basset Griffon Vendeens kindly verified the true scent. All but a few disbelievers, who headed for the exit, settled down. Claude remained hopelessly unaware of the scandal, plugged nostrils, and protests. After all, this was His Moment.

Claude cleared his throat, twitched his whiskers, swayed his hips, and promptly forgot the title of the first record. There were a few catcalls from the audience. Luckily Junior barked at that point—someone had stepped on his right front paw. The audible association helped. Claude remembered the name.

"O.K., folks; here we go! Our first selection this evening will be 'I Ain't Nothing But a Hound Dog.'" Claude picked up his guitar and started his accompaniment, Elvis style.

The dance floor filled with fans of this oldie but goodie. "Cat of My Dreams," a mellow number, followed. Darling couldn't help but smile when, craning her neck from the door, she saw the more naïve cat-debs quiver in hope of slow-dancing to this romantic tune. Darling recollected when she herself had succumbed to dreamy circumstance. She had been much younger and had humored her beaux in those days. She had even invited one dashing Tom home for a late Friskies' Buffet one summer evening.

That same afternoon, she had spent a good deal of money on beauty pedipaw treatments. Decisively, she had even invested in The New Wave Litter Box. Credit card! Caviar n' crackers, catnip on the rocks, cod à la heartthrob! And to what avail?

Only to be thoroughly disillusioned.

Two days later, her Persian friend had cattily divulged that Prince Tom Charming had been heard serenading the pretty, petulant Manx across the street. Darling's faith in the male gender was so shaken that from that day on, she never allowed herself to be completely smitten again. All relationships would be, and were, strictly on her terms.

Claude then played "Anyday Now" for his feathered friends. At the line, "My wild exotic bird will have flown," the birds became so excited that they flew upwards. An interpretive flight pattern emerged. Miss Rat fell off her ladder, such was the sequence of noise and flutter. In fact, Bobby had to bounce a quartet of toucans who couldn't recapture their composure. They were removed under clamorous protest.

Damon, who had been unsuccessfully trying to escort Stella to the dance floor (she was still quite lost in her state of euphoria), was suddenly acutely aware of a disturbance coming from the left side of the room. Scheherazade was squealing in an outraged, ultra-shrill tone. She was hysterically calling for Preppy, Damon, or (out of sheer desperation) for Midnight. Anyone turning to Midnight for help had to be panicked.

Bobby, regrettably, had just stepped outside for a breath of fresh air. Several squirrels had doused their tails with a particularly pungent perfume that made him start to feel rather faint. However, Preppy was now atop Sharon's head, and Midnight, having reluctantly asked Darling to cover for him, was slinking across the floor. He stopped mid-room when he saw Damon approaching and returned to his cash register at double speed. Sharon was trying to soothe the weeping Scheherazade. Damon, aghast that both waitresses were off-duty, spoke consolingly to the damsel so obviously in distress.

"What's wrong, you sweet thing?" he queried.

"Oh Damon, the most shocking experience of my life has just occurred. I'll never be able to show my face here again. Never!"

Thereupon she plunged into the details of her trauma. It seemed that she had never wanted to pose for a passport photo on those few occasions when travel seemed imminent. The rather shallow reason she had given was that at those times she couldn't do a thing with her hair. Vanity, being overly concerned with appearances, became her mantra. Scheherazade had had no problem admitting that. So she had never ventured abroad— to Europe in general and to Italy specifically. Therefore, she was totally unprepared for "The Pinch" on her derrière* when it happened. And, that's what was causing her distress.

Sharon, a bit more "worldly" having many times been mistakenly squeezed as aforementioned eggplantian produce, was only too aware of this waitressing occupational hazard. Scheherazade, in her pink mini, had bent over to retrieve a dropped spoon and thus received a grandiose pinch from Fredrico, the greyhound, an Italian émigré* whose specialty was Renaissance Art. (Afterwards, it was determined that he was hyper-energized due to having eaten too much pasta. Carried away by linguine!) Meant strictly as a compliment, the gesture totally backfired. He had honestly been amazed at Scheherazade's outburst.

Preppy had finally connected with Bobby, and Fredrico learned the hard way the meaning of the famous maxim, "When in Rome, do as the Romans do." In other words, when in "The Furry Disco," remember your American etiquette—or something to that effect. Midnight, eyes glowering, reluctantly refunded Fredrico's money, right before Bobby pushed (more like shoved) the puzzled hound out the door.

Meanwhile, Scheherazade refused to resume her job till she was supplied with a more modest uniform. She had conveniently forgotten that it was she who had demanded the chic apron. Ingeniously, Damon oversaw the removal of a checkered tablecloth from a cozy table for two, and in Dior* fashion, wrapped the ranting girl in it. It hung down almost touching the floor. It is a given that not many males are intrigued by a short, squat moving game board.

So, calmed at last, and just in time for several patrons were losing their patience, Scheherazade was coaxed back to her duties. Sharon, controlling her "I told you so" urge, snuffed significantly, for the first instant not minding her "second-fiddle" status in the beauty department. Attractiveness did have its drawbacks—at times.

CHAPTER 11

THE EVENING CARRIES ON

However, such is life that by the time another hour had passed, Sharon was once again secretly wishing to be a beauty pig for a day. This forceful desire was rekindled after Charlie, a T.V.-devoted rodent, not fooled by the baggy camouflage, became infatuated with Scheherazade. He proceeded to give her an exorbitant tip, of romaine lettuce no less, visualizing her as one of his future "Angels." Davis, having caught the gist of the conversation, couldn't resist a wolf-whistle, much to Scheherazade's discomfort and Sharon's contempt.

Damon returned to Stella who had used his absence as a time to regroup. She smiled demurely when she saw him approaching, feeling a bit more in control, but with knees still shaking. Then they both focused on the music.

Claude, in deference to the barnyard patrons, was playing a late 70's version of "Skip To My Lou," sung blusterously by Reginald R. Rooster. The dancers became so frenzied that one young goat, quite by chance, swung his partner with such force that his tin cap flew off his head and grazed the proper Miss Sally Sheep's crown. Sally baa-ed her annoyance and slumped off to the powder room to repair her woolly disarray. Whereupon, of course, seven other sheep followed, and seven more, until a line formed in the hallway.

Ultimately, Preppy had to inform Damon that only a few hours after opening, they were already out of talcum powder. Damon's suggestion was to borrow some of Adam's fine sugar which had been ordered specifically for the horses' sweet drinks (sugar cubes being a lot dearer). Prep hoped that this spur of the moment remedy would suffice till the morrow when they could replenish their supplies.

This gambit succeeded until, while smoothing her wool, hoping to impress the dashing buck in the vestibule, one sheep licked off all her talcum. It was delicious. So much so that she began licking the others'. Disdaining to be preened like parrots, an inter-species conflict, these others took great umbrage* at this turn of events and started baa-ing their disapproval. The volume increased to such an extent that the entire non-squeaking section wanted their money back.

This would surely have driven Midnight over the brink—they numbered twenty-seven in all at that time. Darling saved the night by offering the discontented customers a sheepskin apology and promising them two free drinks for their inconvenience. The complainers themselves, thus assuaged, began to feel...er...sheepish.

Miss Rat, on the alert, for she recalled the fable of the wolf in sheep's clothing, felt nauseated with anxiety caused by the distasteful bleating. She vowed on the spot that the next time she had insomnia, she would only count gerbils.

A pair of old English sheepdogs managed to distract and quiet the woolly critters by rounding them into a secluded area and demonstrating the intricate steps of "The Virginia Reel." This proved so successful that throughout the evening, one could see little "off-chute" groups practicing a fanciful footfall or two. Four border collies were boogying in delight as we speak.

Adam had no time for wool-gathering. Due to the taxing tales of woe, he was becoming depressed himself—by osmosis it seemed. The monotonous whining had finally forced him to pour his own drink which, instead of making him forget the world's worries, made them seem magnified tenfold. He felt a foreboding twinge amidst the whoopla.

CHAPTER 12

Adieu

Hard to believe, but it was nearing the bewitching hour of midnight. Stella, realizing that it was now or never, shyly agreed to dance the last dance with Damon. Claude began to play "The Party's Over." The assemblage gathered on and around the dance floor and swooned their goodnights.

The canaries had been lulled to sleep two records ago with "By the Time I Get to be a Phoenix." Heads were tucked under wings. The decorative cacti resembled a one-legged haven. Drowsy or not, the air was replete with a yearning to return again—an encouraging sign.

Claude, with a severe catch in his throat, announced curfew. "Folks, this has been the most glorious night of my life," he murmured. "Take care."

An orderly, albeit tired, exodus followed. One exception was Augie Van Doggie, a brooding Bassett, who had begged for just one more song. He now dragged his ears (and belly) along the floor in a swerving, disheartened manner. His moans were quite embarrassing.

Joseph was leaving with Junior. They were locked into a heated discussion. Junior was asking Joseph for a "buy-line."

"Tennis balls, dumbbells, wooden bars…"

"It's just too sticky a subject," explained Joseph.

"But, my pal, Juice, begged me to…"

Damon escorted Stella to the door and thanked her for a lovely evening. She blushed outrageously—an aardvarkian blush—and swished her tail.

"Oh Damon," she sighed, "this night has been the highlight of my hitherto mundane life."

"The pleasure was all mine," he gallantly retorted. "By the way, did you give your quote to Joseph?"

"Certainly. About an hour ago. I'll recite my lines, if you'd like."

Damon assured her of his undivided attention.

Stella began:

> *"A magical night in the midst of the Real*
> *Helps one accept Life's responsibilities*
> *With a renewed sense of Zeal."*

Damon was astonished at the depth of Stella's perception. He wagged his tail twice and kissed her on the cheek. She told him that she would never wash her face again. And she giggled. And bid him goodnight.

CHAPTER 13

THE WAIT...THE TALLY...THE VERDICT

The entrepreneurs finally double-bolted the door. They assembled in the vestibule to discuss their financial and emotional reckonings. A midnight snack had been prepared, and they would stay up until the morning newspapers (with the crucial reviews) hit the stands. The adrenaline was flowing. In particular, their hopes were focused on California Critters' Entertainment Section. As a bonus, if they were successful, they might even be written up in "The Owl Brothers' Who's Hoo." And that would be something else again!

Darling had arranged the menu. A table was appetizingly

set, food at one end, receipts at the other. There was a delectable nosh for everyone. Three courses in all: sunflower applesauce for birds, veggie loaf for rodents and roo, and chunky casserole for dog and cats. Davis, of a sudden, walked pigeon-toed through the applesauce acting very blasé about it. Preppy was furious. He told Davis that manners were an integral part of accomplishment of any kind.

"Furthermore, Davis," he chastised, "a truly cultured parrot walks down the road to riches, without any shortcuts through his victuals."

Davis responded in a most defensive manner. "I declare, Prep, fervent upheaval causes one to forget dignity. I was recalling the excitement of the evening and didn't look where I was walking. I was preoccupied and..."

A simple "sorry" would have sufficed.

Miss Rat then chimed in with her handy motivational maxims that "logic rules supreme, a tidy paw is the law, a well-groomed feather in any weather," ad infinitum.

Davis waddled off in a huff mumbling something about sensitivity as regards to lack of etiquette. In order to mask his embarrassment, he attacked a pile of paper napkins in his path. In his parrot rip-tear frenzy, he inadvertently grabbed a nearby receipt. Whereupon you-know-who had a fit. Darling calmed Midnight down by reminding him of the carbon copy she had kept.

Damon called them to order and reminded all that Davis was just an innocent youth, yet to dip his tail feathers into life. Bobby asked for more herbs and less philosophy. Claude antagonized Sharon and Scheherazade by asking them to serve him his platter. Infuriated, the two overtired waitresses took their chow to a corner alcove to indulge in peace. Both girls had had enough of the male ego to last a lifetime and then some.

Financially, they had just about broken even, which was encouraging in itself. Damon was conversing privately with Preppy who was animatedly bobbing his head up and down in a glugging fashion. On the whole, it was a tense scene. Even Adam had his right paw raised as his involuntary response to the agitation in the air. His understanding nature evaporated around contention. Damon hoped that this opening night stress would soon dissipate.

The animals began their vigil. Their tummies were full, their psyches exhausted, and their limbs weary. Strain overruled all else.

At 5:30 a.m., the reviews were out. Joseph himself came running to hand deliver the hot-off-the-press copy. Damon turned to the entertainment page with shaking paws. He yipped for joy! "The Furry Disco" was an unconditional triumph! Four stars all the way: ambiance, diversion, refreshment, and service! And, as the crowning glory, Sir William Venerable the Third, the visiting English Bulldogue dignitary, was delaying his departure one day—at the State Department's expense, of course—to visit this new night club.

The critters cheered! Their dream had come true! In fact, it was several hours before any of these over-stimulated animals were able to unwind and catch some shut-eye. Their eyelids twitched with visions of delight. Their collective cup runneth over so to speak (and ranneth into a current of…).

CHAPTER 14

TIME PASSES

Now, if the reader bear with me (no pun intended), I shall pause in the narrative, only to continue six months later—the same scene, a kindred Friday.

The time can be pinpointed at 8:00 p.m., corroborated by Porcupine Pete. The latter had been mistaken one evening for a decorative sagebrush and was locked in at closing by dint of natural camouflage. Talk about fortuitous. He was subsequently hired as a substitute for Bobby during his breaks. Anyone who has ever been approached by a walking pincushion is familiar with the apprehension evoked by the sight. And, needless to say, when it came to curfew, his quills never failed, only his temper.

Many changes had transpired in this half year, the least of which was financial. To be succinct, dollars had arrived, and common sense had departed. The metamorphosis* had started slowly, and as is sometimes the case, had built up in momentum until all restraint had been relinquished. Although the disco vibes remained the same—neon glitter, resonant music—the inner souls of the critters had become tainted.

Damon, for one, could be seen, tail between his legs in disapproval, pacing around the disco with Preppy as his only confidant. Prep, head cocked to one side, riding on Damon's shoulder, lent a kindly ear to Damon's lamentations punctuated by low woofs. Preppy echoed his whines in an unhappy, though perfect, imitation.

In contrast, however, the other entrepreneurs, quite oblivious to Damon's mood, strutted about gesticulating, gloating, and grasping. It was as if a fun house with a hall of mirrors had been installed. The gang seemed to have become a distortion of what they had once been.

Claude's amour propre* had emerged into bona fide egomania. At this very moment, he was badgering Miss Rat about renaming "The Furry Disco." He felt that "Chez Claude" would better suit their purpose.

Miss Rat calmly queried, "Why, oh why, Mr. Record Spinner, do you think that you have become Mr. Record Maker?"

"Gee whiz, Miss Rat, you know that my choices are superb, oriented magnificently to individual and group consciousness…"

"Oh, come off your high horse." (Miss Rat quickly looked

around to see if any equine had overheard her slip of the lip.) "And, to be perfectly blunt, Claude, several of your 'live' renditions of the week's Top Ten are for the birds!" This second inter-species blooper, in so short a time, made Miss Rat abruptly end the conversation. She needed to hang upside down and clear her head. Immediately.

The truth of the matter was that Claude was so caught up in his own charisma, that he didn't realize that his performances, witticisms, and the like were barely discernible amidst the noise and wonder of being seen in the ritzy disco. Claude's groupies, especially the Himalayans and Burmese, screamed for attention and tried to rip out a whisker or two for souvenir. He realized that certain inconveniences came with the territory. Therefore, he chose to block out the effects of "mob psychology." (Youngsters, to simplify the latter phraseology, think of it as one cheer, many cheers, one shriek, many shrieks, anything goes when lost in the crowd…) He just gloried in the fame.

Miss Rat had earnestly tried to explain that hysteria of any sort should be terminated or rerouted as quickly as possible. Especially adoring applause. She had reiterated that Claude should not let his head be turned by mindless cause and effect or stimulus and response. He had just shrugged and, like Narcissus* before him, gazed in the mirror and complacently purred.

Midnight came puffing by. He had gained a total of ten pounds in approximately 180 days. As he tried to squeeze past Claude, he bumped into him. Then Midnight had to endure a tirade of verbal abuse about messing-up the star's appearance, right before the next performance. Midnight forebore to engage in repartée* since his spunk was quite defused by excess poundage. For Midnight had decided that waistline was secondary to the joys of gluttony*. He had consistently gorged himself on salmon, tuna, shrimp, and soft-shell crabs. One could say that, to date, he had literally eaten his earnings.

Midnight seemed unconcerned that his former sinister appearance had been dispelled by fat. Slinking across the floor had become more of a waggling, and he exuded less of black magic and more of mellow pudding. Sly had become anti-spry; voodooism had been outdistanced by culinary hedonism*. So be it! Midnight refused to surrender his new-found rights to daily fish splurges. Miss Rat had everyone calling him "P.S.," for Paunchy Smarty-Pants, at every opportunity in hopes of bringing him to his senses.

CHAPTER 15

THE DOWNWARD SPIRAL CONTINUES

Darling, observing the interchange between Claude and Midnight, called them "immature peasants" to their faces. Having thus rebuked them, she spat twice and disdainfully walked away. To tell the truth, Darling had resisted her own personal temptation for one entire month. Then she had given in to the cult of haute couture*.

At the onset, a cursory glance at the dress collars had been more obligatory than in-depth study. However, after the more affluent patrons became part of the disco scene, the glitter of diamond-studded bands overwhelmed her dormant female consciousness. Her nonchalant* attitude towards stylish attire did a 360 degree. Instead of a trip to better bitter cat conditions for single felines in the southwest, Chanel, Calvin Klein, and Dior showings received top priority. Airline tickets to Paris graced her desk. She had even started taking French lessons! Darling was now referred to as "la chatte à la mode*."

Then too, she had begun hanging around "The Persians Pompous," an afternoon gregarious group devoted to the promotion of *Glamour Puss* magazine. Darling had moved from social awareness to social pretentiousness in record time.

"Hey, Adam, like my new necklace?" asked Darling.

Adam, who in all honesty totally disliked her new image, didn't bother answering. His head hung low; his entire body language indicated depression. Being timid had been a strain; being timid and saddened was just too much. Six months of hard-luck stories, complaints, and distorted anecdotes had gotten to him.

Damon had not been surprised when he found out that Adam would require an immediate raise because he had started going to thrice-weekly therapy sessions. Trying to make light of the situation, Damon jokingly commented that a cat doesn't use a couch for counseling, only for sharpening! Adam, who had just that morning had his claws clipped, didn't find the remark a bit funny—especially since the caticurist had jested in a similar vein.

Adopting a graver tone, Damon questioned Adam about his therapist's techniques—eliminating, of course, the more purrsonal details. Dr. Von Sigmund, a Standard Schnauzer who had studied in Vienna, was considered to be the best "shrink" in the west. After the initial session, devoted to easing the "held-up-front-paw" syndrome, Dr. Siggy knew that all his skills would have to be brought into play. In the space of fifty minute intervals, Adam was taken from Freud to "Simon Says," from childhood to dreams, and from Gestalt* to ink blots. His paw, at this particular time was immobilized in the air.

"You must have extreme difficulty pouring the drinks, mmm?" queried Siggy.

"I…I've gotten used to it—but oh docteur, I k…keep h… having a recurring nightmare."

"And that is, Adam?" mumbled Siggy in his renowned soothing tone.

"I'm at 'The Furry Disco' and Claude spins this record—a record of nonstop country-style woes. It drones on and on accompanied by a quartet of fiddles in the background. I ask… er…beseech Claude to change the record. He laughs and keeps replaying the same one while saying 'by popular demand'…"

Dr. Siggy tugged at his beard and shook his ears. "Easy now, Adam. We'll try hypnosis next week. Sorry, your time is up."

"So you see, Damon," Adam concluded, "at fifty dollars an hour, I'm flat broke."

Damon did see. He was saved from commenting by the flamboyant entrance of Sharon and Scheherazade. The girls scurried past blowing bubbles and popping their chewing gum. They had become twin rah-rah cheerleader types—"Valley Girls"—totally awfully awesome! Their little derrières swished, their faces were caked with maquillage*, and pink blush highlighted their cheekbones.

Unfortunately, in reality, Sharon looked like a garish eggplant. An eccentric ellipsoid entity! In like manner, Scheherazade, with trendy braided hair, would have been rated a negative ten on a Bo Derek* scale. She had taken "cute" to a new level, even ordering her cardboard boxes in passion pink. And, much to Miss Rat's dismay, had color-coordinated her food! Purple parsley is a rather disconcerting sight whether it matches an accessory or not.

But, who would notice in this self-absorbed environment? The feather lobby had become so flighty that it would take more than baby-blue lettuce to cause a flutter.

Only Damon, Preppy, and Miss Rat of the original associates had maintained their perspectives. They, at least, still had their priorities straight.

Meanwhile, Davis (now a full-time employee) unfailingly overdosed on sunflower seed, sang upside down clinging to any and every available surface, and repeating, in an irritating monotone, his newly-voiced slogan:

"Fun, fun for everyone
Fun, fun has just begun."

Davis's eyes were glazed with visions of corn on the cob, sliced apple, and squash. He was too "seeded" most of the time to wolf-whistle at all anymore, if such had been his inclination.

In fact, Davis's "seediness" was vexing Bobby, who had lost most of his buoyancy. Bob wanted "fun" removed from all dictionaries, everywhere. He had just secretly reapplied to Qantas. He figured anything was better than the position he was in now. The disco was always packed to capacity. Come what may, Damon would have to hire at least four more "roos" in order to keep the peace. He, Bobby, had bounced off several pounds, and his former formidable image had become rather skeletal. And, poor Adam's nerves were strung so tautly that Bobby was having an impossible time distinguishing a true skirmish from a false alarm. Edginess seemed the order of the day.

So Success—with a capital "S"—had turned, in a philosophical sense, into a Catastrophe—with a capital "C." Since the situation was not by any means limited to felines, perhaps we should call it "Animalstrophe"—with a capital "A." The meaningless merriment cycle seemed destined to continue forever, weakening that which was decent and endearing in the hearts of these critters. They were just a handful to be sure, but one could consider them a cross-section of animalkind. A microcosm*, at that!

Sharon

Claude

Scheherazade

CHAPTER 16

It Begins

We are now pinpointed at 8:30 p(orcupine) m(eridian), ergo the customers were flocking in. It was the long-awaited half year anniversary gala. Catnip punch was about to flow for the revelers, spring water for the more subdued. In more ways than one, it was another "happening," as well as reunion for the pioneer opening-nighters.

The noise level was decibels above usual, and the activity at the door had quickened. Midnight and Darling were momentarily inundated with arrivals, which led to a grievous oversight: they admitted a minor to the party. The silky beige guinea pig in question—Ashley by name—had flurried by in a wave of white chiffon. She had flashed an "I.D." while squealing maturely. She had had her paw stamped and scuttled to the bar.

Ashley tried to mesh herself with a neighboring group of cavies. Adam became suspicious when she did not know how to order and stumbled by asking for a "bottle of mil...mint juice." He signaled Preppy, who in turn informed Damon.

"Young lady," Damon began.

"Yes, sir," quivered Ashley.

"Miss, how old are you?"

"I...I'm...I forget, sir."

Ashley couldn't continue the charade. She burst into tears.

Damon gently escorted her back to the door, and with a glare at Darling, told Ash she might return in a year or two. As a kind gesture, to alleviate her embarrassment, Damon offered a watercress sandwich to go, "on the house."

Ash was so inexperienced that she told Damon she was not yet allowed to climb stairs or go under or on top of the house. Damon sighed patiently and motioned to Miss Rat. He knew she would be able to help. As he returned to his duties, Damon overheard Miss Rat begin, at the way beginning, with "raining cats and dogs." Ash was having her first lesson in figurative speech.

The dancing had begun, and the festivities were in full swing, when a dozen raccoons, asking for a group rate, sought admittance. Midnight rapidly calculated a suitable group discount and shooed them in. He told Darling that this could be the commencement of branching out into catered private functions. Darling, admiring her recently purchased gold anklet, nodded absent-mindedly in assent. Neither cat would ever have dreamed, amidst the high degree of frolicking, that the revelment was about to come to an unanticipated halt.

CHAPTER 17

OH NO!

At this point, I feel compelled to warn any reader, under the age of eight, to seek out an older sibling or adult as we relate the unforeseen turn of events that was to follow.

Claude was crooning, the patrons were swaying, and the lights were flashing, when violence reared its ugly head. Since Joseph was at the disco and journalism is his forte, I will quote his eyewitness account verbatim. His column made the front page in California Critter the following morning. So goes the sinister scenario.

* * *

"Mafia* Syndicate Hits Furry Disco!"

11:05 p.m. Only the more astute would have been aware of the coordinated movement deviously orchestrated by the raccoons. Two advanced north, two south, two east, two west, two to the bar, and two near the door. It was a synchronized ballet of deliberate dupery executed on stealthy tiptoe.

11:15 p.m. Coon hands, in black leather gloves, withdraw sham pistols in unison. Customers and employees are asked to "freeze." All complied. One shivering whippet who initially thought this was an ill-timed stunt began a somewhat chilly retort. He stopped mid-sentence when he realized what was afoot, or in this case ahand, and that humor, sarcastic or not, wouldn't be appropriate or safe.

11:25 p.m. The leader, Rocky C., informed all that no one would be hurt if the following conditions were met:

1. Midnight, hand over cash.
2. Darling, collect dress collars and bands.
3. Scheherazade and Sharon, relinquish all tips, leafy or coin.
4. Miss Rat, waive her new instamatic camera received as gift from her suitor, Whiskers.
5. Davis, amass all sunflower seeds, fruit, and miscellaneous treats.

6-7. Stella and Junior, give up evening ant pouch and bag of sticks respectively.

8. Bobby, spring forward to be tied and gagged.
9. Claude, say goodbye to his guitar, boots, hat, and solid gold records.
10. Adam, be revived, for he had fainted at the onset of the robbery. Thereafter serve the rowdy dozen catnip beverages so they could toast their successful plunder.
11-12. Preppy and Damon, surrender their priceless Beagles' record, symbol of "The Furry Disco" itself. Then, and only then, would everyone's safety be assured.

A dozen disastrous demands by a dozen deceitful derelicts. Rocky had had the list Xeroxed and offered one copy to Damon and another to Joseph after he finished reading the terms aloud. Obviously this was a well-planned caper and not a harried heist.

11:35 p.m. The villainous twelve supervised the mobilization.

11:55 p.m. The nefarious deed accomplished, the coons backed out of the disco, their knapsacks filled to overflowing. Their innate facial masks served to accentuate the malefic. Damon shared that he knew it would be a challenge for sleuths at "Paws Unlimited" to solve this crime.

* * *

By 12:30 a.m. the disco's occupants had gathered their wits about them—more or less. There were a wit or two still obscured in a corner, huddling together for security. (Miss Rat, we've gone figurative again.) One could honestly state that everyone was stressed to the max. In the duration of an hour, an all-American dream had been shattered.

CHAPTER 18

THE IMMEDIATE AFTERMATH

Damon, head mournfully between his paws, kept sighing, while Preppy flew repetitively back and forth between the now vacant place of honor over the bar and Damon's shoulder, as if to reaffirm that he indeed had not been having a nightmare. Claude, for the first time unconcerned with his "public," was crying unabashedly for his missing treasures. It had, after all, taken him three months to break in those cowboy boots. Midnight and Darling, paws wrapped consolingly around each other's neck, were lamenting their material losses.

As Midnight succinctly phrased it, "No wealth; no worth!"

To which Darling added, "No jewelry; no jubilance!"

So engrossed in their woes were these felines, it fell to

Adam to untie and ungag Bobby, the latter having been shoved ingloriously into the broom closet at the farthest corner of the room. As Adam laboriously undid knot after knot, it flashed through his mind how foolish he had been to be Depressed—with a capital "D," before a truly traumatic Event—with a capital "E" had taken place. It took him quite a while to free Bobby since he had to use only one paw. The sad fact was that his other front one was completely paralyzed from this bewildering incident. His raccoon-demanded drinks had been poured half in glasses, half on the counter. Moreover, he had only been able to satisfy his "orders" because two mastiffs supported him, under each pawpit, on either side. Luckily these two gents had been seated at the bar at crime time.

Meanwhile, Davis was having difficulty in convincing the birds to remove their heads from under their wings. After taunting:

> *"Ostrich, ostrich,*
> *Ho, ho, ho.*
> *You look so comical,*
> *with heads buried so,"*

he managed to insult a pair of the true big "O's" who had come specifically to enter the dance contest. The flustered fowl didn't deign to respond to the chaff. Nevertheless, when a glass broke in the background, the jittery birds finally looked up. Heads emerged. However, panic-induced laryngitis had struck en masse* so the usual twitterings were absent. It was far too quiet.

Davis, trying to liven things up again, emitted a resounding wolf-whistle. Whereupon, Scheherazade and Sharon threw their pom-poms at him and rushed to search for their plain, old, grey cardboard box. They were longing for a feeling of security. En route, they passed Miss Rat who was trying to derive a logical moral from this illogical madness. She wanted to offer a degree of solace to the disoriented critters. Somehow, all she could think of was "the cheese stands alone" which seemed to have no meaning in the present context.

"What cheese, Miss Rat?" asked Whiskers.

"Oh, did I say cheese? I meant thieves; see, they rhyme."

Whiskers decided not to mention the plural inconsistency.

He was trying to be a gentleman rat (also studiously avoiding mention of their lost camera). He had been wooing and humoring Miss Rat for several months. He could not hazard heartbreak. "I sort of understand," he mumbled.

"Well, the thieves stand alone with our loot!" After which, she wrapped her tail around her elbow and stumbled off, lost in the recesses of her mind, trying to create sense out of a senseless situation.

It was a doleful time. The dejected patrons departed parade-like led by a weeping Junior, reciting his poignant "Ode to a Stick." Acting as the caboose, Stella dragged home. She had made up her mind that Life was a compromise. Henceforth, all her efforts would be slanted towards remarriage and calm. Romance, and its pursuit, was simply too unnerving an experience. She would join "Aardvarks Without Partners" in the morning.

In point of fact, and verified by Pete, the only happy personage was Joseph. He, as spectator to this scoop, would wow his editor-in-chief, never to be the newsroom "gopher" again. With all due respect to his panda soul, Joe did feel a twinge of guilt that his good fortune had been created out of his friends' misfortune. But, to quote Miss Rat, "C'est la vie*!"

Meanwhile, Damon dialed the emergency hot-line of "Paws Unlimited." The agency promised to send out their top blood-hounds—Sleuth One and Sleuth Two—immediately. It was

1:00 a.m. Only two hours had passed. Yet the carefree mood of the early evening seemed ages ago.

CHAPTER 19

AND MORE SO—THE GRILLING

Sadly, come what may, it could not be denied that an irrevocable blow had been dealt individually and collectively to the furry discoites. They all knew that the disco itself would have to be closed indefinitely. Theft insurance would barely cover about one-third of their monetary loss. Then too, there was that other issue. If nothing else, Damon was totally superstitious and would not even consider reopening till his Beagles' record was found. He was not one to tempt fate.

Psychologically, they were ravaged. It was if an almighty needle had burst their bubble. Suddenly, they were acutely self-conscious and regarded one another, uncomfortably, as strangers. Everyone was tired and distraught. There was a noted lack of reaction when the Sleuths arrived.

Preppy wondered if the interrogation could be postponed 'til the morrow. His soul had been touched by Claude, who had donned an old beret in the interim, in a half-hearted attempt to regain his poise. Prep handed him a bowtie found under a chair earlier that night. It was a poor substitute for his dandy bandana. However, Claude's psyche notwithstanding, Prep reluctantly had to agree with Damon and the detectives that questioning had to start while the crime scene was fresh in the mind…

The inquiry began.

First, all the key witnesses were seated at separate tables, so they could not talk to, and thereby influence, one another. Sleuth One and Two began taking statements at different ends of the room. They were going to try their best to uncover clues which would lead to the arrest of the callous, culpable coons. Their only leads so far were a few smudged pawprints—most likely the result of Sharon's dropping of her tray when she had realized what was happening. Said impressions were taken from the wet spots on the floor.

The Sherlock Hounds doggedly questioned the bystanders. The incredible variance in the replies made the two feel that they were delving into several unrelated burglaries instead of just one.

Darling swore that the leader had exceptionally long, coarse reddish-brown hair and that the majority of the curs were rather unkempt. Strangely enough, she had actually advised

Midnight not to accept their dollars. Bad aura. However, in his greed, Midnight had retorted that their "fishy" group image was "pseudo-hippie" by design. Role-playing for an evening! He was sure. He would not be "de-caviared" by a petty, suspicious circumstance.

Adam had noticed that about half of the coons had buck teeth. He, himself, could not help recommending orthodontia treatment when they had initially been nibbling on the hors-d'oeuvres.

Damon had found their scent extremely acrid. "Still, detective," he explained, "the ongoing raccoon...er...dog controversy may have colored my judgment."

"Would you please be more specific," demanded Sleuth One.

"Okay, look at it this way. When the coons entered the disco, I bent over backwards..."

"Straining his right shoulder," interrupted Preppy.

"...to be super-courteous," concluded Damon.

"I see—a sensitive area," the bloodhound agreed and promptly altered his line of inquiry.

Sleuth Two began waving his paw excitedly. Claude had just furnished him with a concrete lead. He remembered that one of the raccoons had a white, star-shaped birthmark right before the first ring on his tail.

"How can you be so positive, Claude?" asked Two.

"Really! This particular raccoon swaggered in like a 'hot-shot,' enamored with his own being. You couldn't miss him." (Isn't it remarkable how one can recognize vanity in others and not be aware of this very same weakness in self?)

Claude had disliked him on the spot—recognizing a potential adversary. He didn't share this last with the detective, for obvious reasons.

Preppy noticed that three of the raccoons had earrings in their ears, and that the smallest of the trio wore an unusual watchband. Prep was certain that it was stolen or "hot" merchandise. He had heard about it from a "fence" group—three ravens. In fact, there had been a recent flurry of nocturnal pilfering of valuables, specifically jewelry with inlaid designs and semi-precious stones.

Scheherazade and Sharon found the interrogation very embarrassing. Both girls had received swim party invitations from two raccoon dudes. The latter had had the audacity to whisper the invites during the actual heist itself. "Hey, cuties, you and us can have a very unique time."

Their grammar had been fifth grade level at tops. Sharon had been doubly astounded when her suitor had insisted, "Come with me, Hon; you'll do real good."

"Is that as rewarding as doing really well?" she had retorted.

The sarcasm completely escaped the bandit.

The other witnesses were ineffectual. In sum, they declared that one raccoon looked just like another and only a "mama" could know for sure. I refuse to bore the reader with any "masked" allusions. The only deduction to be drawn was that it would be a lengthy, tedious investigation.

Before long, Sleuth One and Two called it a night. They

puckered up their rolls of flab and departed with noses to the ground, in the hopes of appearing to have an especial plan in mind. The fatigued entrepreneurs crashed on the floor, too tired to even go home.

"An unforgettable night," summarized Damon, not living up to his usual mastery of the English language.

CHAPTER 20

INSIGHT

Now I could prolong this narrative indefinitely and weave my way through issues of rededication, reconstruction, and even refinancing. However, I feel that the unadulterated truth must, as the eagle, come to light. Volumes have been written on catharsis, shock, or day of reckoning—call it what you will. For whatever misfortunes the robbery had produced, it had also provided Damon's group with a shattering insight into their own spiritual deterioration.

They disliked that which they observed in their comrades. And, they disliked that which they saw in themselves. Gone were altruistic motives; collapsed was commitment; tarnished was the very meaning of friendship. It had been quite a while since a helping paw was offered to Feather or Fur in need.

Dispersed were animaltarian goals of equality. What had evolved was an "eat-drink-preen-enrich" merry-go-round. A calliope of fame, greed, and self-aggrandizement! Understanding had vanished.

It was not surprising that Damon's black spots, in the space of merely those one hundred eighty some-odd days, had become tinged with grey. Long-discarded was his once feared demerit system. The critters had begun to laugh at this old-fashioned, silly penalty. "I'll do as I please" echoed everywhere. In other words, a lot of heads had been turned. An occasional observant owl or two (who, in due respect, were used to above-neck contortions) noted that only three of the partners had remained immune to successmania. They knew hoo. Damon, Prep, and Miss Rat!

Preppy, realizing that Damon was resembling his late grandfather more each day, made it his business to become the lackluster dog's inseparable companion post-robbery. Preppy chattered incessantly into his ear, alternating from left to right for variety. Miss Rat hung upside down, whiskers twitching in pique. She had realized long ago that unleashed prosperity logically ends in psychic defeat. Oddly enough, it had taken a foul felony to bring the situation to a head.

The time had come to start anew.

CHAPTER 21

REGENERATION

The critters recouped that which they could. A unanimous decision transformed the disco into a non-profit recreational foundation. All proceeds were to help foster after-school sports for the town's youth. Nevertheless, recognizing the allure of parties, bi-monthly dances were scheduled wherein the entrepreneurs could resume their former disco posts (save Bobby who had returned home) for old times' sake.

Adam could pour the punch with two paws now that his melancholy had lifted, and the crowds had thinned. He was one of those who just never worked well under pressure. His only concession to the past, so to speak, was to have Porcupine Pete stationed at his feet during the drink serving. That way he could distinguish a mere twinge of anxiety and banish it immediately. Dr. Siggy would have been proud.

Midnight promised to help with any sleight of hand entertainment, (ah, it's a relief to rediscover former beloved hobbies!) but only after the first month or two. He had to live the life of a recluse for awhile because of his determination to adhere to a strict diet. It had taken the jeers of two junior high felines, mocking his shape, to make Midnight realize that there was not more of him to admire, but more of him to ridicule. In time, he would come to think of it as working on his own disappearing act.

Sharon and Scheherazade could be seen every afternoon with their Organic Gardening textbooks under their paws. Their immediate goal was a B.S. in Horticulture. But, such was their enthusiasm, a Master's Degree and a Ph.D. were not out of the question. Their get-up-and-go had been wisely rerouted. They were the cutest coeds around.

Darling had burned her *Glamour Puss* magazine collection (the press had had a field day with that) and had become chair-feline of The AAUWC (American Association of University Women Cats). Their first luncheon, specifically benefiting timorous tortoise shells who spend their time in the cupboard, was to be held in three weeks, all returns going to the "Felines in Distress Hotline." Darling was liberated again, both figuratively and literally. Nowadays, she wore nothing around her neck; she had felt a little bare at first but knew for a fact that collars, of any kind, bind. I'm certain that you will hear of Darling's crusades in the future issues of *California Critter*. Joseph has interviewed her twice already.

Davis hung around Claude and wolf-whistled every time the former D.J. began to exhibit any narcissistic mannerism. It was their secret code. In effect, this became a perfect arrangement. Claude began to show more discretion in his choice of wardrobe, although he was never seen without his cowboy footwear. Davis kept Claude's new whisker comb with his avian cakes, and Regeneration afforded him limited access. This restricted Claude's self-pampering.

Claude thought it was so neat to have his own purrsonal side-kick that he was writing an original song, à la Willie Nelson*, for Davis. Even if it bombed, it was an exciting project. It was a positive focus.

And, Damon, mentor of the community, aware from the start that pleasure should never usurp reason, had his tail raised high once more.

Damon—the learned one! Only he had been present the night that Preppy had flown back with his Beagles' record and buried it in the bottom drawer of the dresser under his rainwear. Damon had poured his friend a glass of apple juice, himself one of milk, and the Dynamic Duo had toasted one another. They would remain blood brothers to the end, bound in secrecy, bird and dog!

You see, sometimes a Dalmatian has to take charge—even if it means doing something a wee bit controversial. Only Preppy had witnessed Damon's exchange of cash (rinsed by twelve pair of paws to check its authenticity) on the dock, a week after the robbery. It had been a dark and stormy night...

But, Philosophers have been known to throw caution to the wind in order to succor—or lend a helping paw to—Society.

Yet, Damon was more than content to return to a placid, meditative existence once more. If you call him, and no one answers, check the picnic table out back. He'll be there, sniffing the air, totally engrossed in his continuing search for the true meaning of His Spot on Earth.

The End, although...

THE FURRY DISCO GLOSSARY

à la mode (Fr.): *adj.* stylish

albinism: *n.* the state of lacking normal pigmentation

amour propre (Fr.): *n.* respect for oneself, self esteem

Annie Oakley: star sharpshooter in Buffalo Bill's Wild West Show

avuncular: *adj.* pertaining to an uncle

Bo Derek: movie star rated a perfect 10 for beauty

cache: *n.* a hiding place for storing provisions

C'est la vie (Fr.): "such is life"

Christian Dior: French fashion designer

collateral: *n.* property used as security to show sincerity in fulfilling an agreement

Dear John: *n.* a letter as to a service man requesting a divorce or ending a personal relationship

derrière (Fr.): *n.* the rear

émigré: *n.* one who leaves a native country to settle some where else

en masse (Fr): *adj.* "all together"

entrepreneur: *n.* one who launches a business venture, often assuming risks

façade: *n.* an artificial or deceptive pretense.

faux pas (Fr.): *n.* a social blunder, a mistake

Florence Nightingale: British nurse, founder of modern nursing

Freudian: *n.* a follower of the theories of Sigmund Freud, who developed psychoanalysis—the method of psychiatric therapy in which free association, dream interpretation, etc. are used to cure anxieties

Gestalt: *n.* the theory in psychology that compares the importance of the whole to the sum of the parts

gluttony: *n.* eating to excess

haute couture (Fr.): *n.* high fashion

hedonism: *n.* a way of life devoted to the pursuit of pleasure

laissez-faire (Fr.): *n.* non-interference

Mafia: *n.* an alleged international criminal organization

malathion: *n.* an organic phosphate insecticide with low toxicity to plants and animals

maquillage (Fr.): *n.* cosmetic or theatrical make-up

martyrdom: *n.* one who makes a great sacrifice to advance a belief, cause or principle

metamorphosis: *n.* change or transformation

microcosm: *n.* the universe in miniature, a little world

Midas: a fabled king who received the power of turning to gold all that he touched

Narcissus: a youth who fell in love with his own image

nonchalant: *adj.* seeming to be coolly indifferent

pedestrian: *adj.* undistinguished, ordinary

queue: *n.* a tail; *v.* to form a line (usually used with up)

raison d'être: *n.* reason for existing

repartée (Fr.): *n.* a swift, witty reply

rhetoric: *n.* the art of persuasive language

serendipity: *n.* the knack for discovering desirable things accidentally

Shangri-La: *n.* an imaginary paradise on Earth

stoicism: *n.* indifference to pleasure or pain

terra firma (Lat.): *n.* solid ground

umbrage: *n.* resentment (to take umbrage)

vociferous: *adj.* noisy and insistent

Willie Nelson: popular country western singer

ABOUT THE AUTHOR

A New Yorker by birth, **Jo Kearley** taught for over 30 years. She is retired now—to the delight of her critters. Her "raison d'être," her passion, has always been the love of animals. Her personal menagerie denizens were the inspiration behind the composite characters in *The Furry Disco*.

About the Editor

A Californian by birth, **Stephanie Chan**, a former 4th and 5th grade student of Ms. Kearley's, teaches English and Literature. She studied at UC Berkeley, San Jose State University, and UC Santa Cruz where she completed a dissertation focusing on race in ethnic American literature and popular culture. A point to note is that when in 5th grade, Stephanie received the Student of Year Award. Ms. Kearley called her "the wind beneath her wings."

ABOUT THE ILLUSTRATOR

First grade teaching assistant, lower school art teacher at Old Orchard School, **Russell Powell** is a gifted artist and creator of technique called "hand stamping." He too is one of Ms. Kearley's former students. His sketching abilities are astounding and his hand-stamp paintings are becoming an worldwide internet sensation. Follow him on Instagram/pangaeanstudios

www.ingramcontent.com/pod-product-compliance
Lightning Source LLC
Chambersburg PA
CBHW070633130626
46555CB00006B/2538